THIS IS THE TEACHER

by **Rhonda Gowler Greene**

illustrated by **Mike Lester**

SCHOLASTIC INC.
New York   Toronto   London   Auckland   Sydney
Mexico City   New Delhi   Hong Kong   Buenos Aires

ISBN 0-439-81550-9

Text copyright © 2004 by Rhonda Gowler Greene.
Illustrations copyright © 2004 by Mike Lester. All rights reserved.
Published by Scholastic Inc., 557 Broadway, New York, NY 10012,
by arrangement with Dutton Children's Books, a member of
Penguin Group (USA) Inc. SCHOLASTIC and associated logos are
trademarks and/or registered trademarks of Scholastic Inc.

12 11 10 9 8 7 6 5 4 3 2 1   5 6 7 8 9 10/0

Printed in the U.S.A.   08

This edition first printing, September 2005

Designed by Irene Vandervoort

Aa Bb Cc Dd

This is the teacher all ready for school.

These are the students who rush through the door,
who drop sacks of lunches that **smash!** on the floor
and topple the teacher all ready for school.

This is the ant farm that spilled—**oh, my!**—

on top of the desk with the tissue supply

by the students who rushed

and toppled the teacher all ready for school.

This is the snake brought for show-and-tell time
that snuck from its shoe box and slithered and climbed
toward the ants that were spilled
by the students who rushed
and toppled the teacher all ready for school.

This is the girl with the red, runny nose
who shrieked at the ants crawling inside her clothes
and the long snake that climbed
toward the ants that were spilled
by the students who rushed
and toppled the teacher all ready for school.

These are the cupcakes that flew through the air

when the birthday boy slipped and tripped over the chair

of the scared girl who shrieked

at the long snake that climbed

toward the ants that were spilled

by the students who rushed

and toppled the teacher all ready for school.

This is the loose tooth that fell down the drain
and got stuck—*ker-plink!*—so the janitor came
and slid on some cake
by the scared girl who shrieked
at the long snake that climbed
toward the ants that were spilled
by the students who rushed
and toppled the teacher all ready for school.

This is the bad bee that buzzed through the crack,
then zoomed round the room in a stinging attack
as the raindrops fell—*plop!*
after—*whack!*—the ball soared
near the room where they munched
and—**Eek!** There's that hamster that spins in a wheel!

This is the fountain that made a huge lake
when its drain was clogged by the show-and-tell snake
as the bad bee went *buzz*
and the raindrops fell—*plop!*
after—*whack!*—the ball soared
near the room where they munched
and—**Eek!** There's that hamster that spins in a wheel!

This is the kid who got sick that day,

so the janitor came with a mop and some spray

by the fountain that clogged

as the bad bee went *buzz*

and the raindrops fell—*plop!*

after—*whack!*—the ball soared

near the room where they munched

and—**Eek!** There's that hamster that spins in a wheel!

This is the mural they made with a *splash!*

and—yikes!—caused the paint cans to teeter and *crash!*

near the kid who got sick

by the fountain that clogged

as the bad bee went *buzz*

and the raindrops fell—*plop!*

after—*whack!*—the ball soared

near the room where they munched

and—Eek! There's that hamster that spins in a wheel!

This is the line where they stand, tall and straight,
knowing tomorrow they'll be back by eight
to march by the mural they made with a *splash!*

This is the teacher with books in a bag

who walks from the building, beneath the tall flag,

leading the line

past the mural they made

near the kid who got sick

by the fountain that clogged

as the bad bee went *buzz*

and the raindrops fell—*plop!*

after—*whack!*—the ball soared

near the room where they munched

and that hamster that hid

by the books that fell—**oops!**—

near the tooth that was found

and the cupcakes that flew

by the scared girl who shrieked

at the long snake that climbed

toward the ants that were spilled

by the students who rushed

and toppled the teacher . . .

. . . all ready for bed!